The Lighthouse Keeper's Breakfast

Ronda and David Armitage

To Alan and Oliver

Scholastic Children's Books,
Commonwealth House, 1-19 New Oxford Street,
London WC1A 1NU, UK
a division of Scholastic Ltd

London ~ New York ~ Toronto ~ Sydney ~ Auckland
Mexico City ~ New Delhi ~ Hong Kong

First published by Scholastic Ltd, 2000

Text copyright © Ronda Armitage, 2000
Illustrations copyright © David Armitage, 2000

ISBN 0 439 01350 X

Typeset in Baskerville MT Schoolbook

Printed in China

All rights reserved

2 4 6 8 10 9 7 5 3 1

The rights of Ronda and David Armitage to be identified as the author
and illustrator of this work respectively have been asserted by them in
accordance with the Copyright, Designs and Patents Act, 1988.

The Lighthouse Keeper's Breakfast

by

Ronda and David Armitage

SCHOLASTIC
PRESS

Mr and Mrs Grinling lived with their cat, Hamish, in a little white cottage perched high on the cliffs. Mr Grinling was a lighthouse keeper. By day and night, with his assistant Sam, he lovingly tended the light.

One Wednesday morning when Sam was polishing, he noticed a tiny inscription right at the top of the lighthouse.
"Well, well," he said to himself. "Just fancy that!"

"Our lighthouse is 200 years old this year," he told everyone.

"We should celebrate," said Mrs Grinling.

"Maybe some presents," said Mr Grinling. "A fresh coat of red and white paint."

"And a party," said Mrs Grinling.

"How about fancy dress?" suggested Sally de la Croissant, the baker.

"Something to do with the sea," said Jason the postman. "I've got a lovely octopus suit."

"We can use my old sailing ship," roared Admiral Fleetabix,
"I'll moor her out in the bay."
"Can it be an all night party with a birthday breakfast?"
asked the children. "It is an extremely important occasion."
And everyone agreed that Mr and Mrs Grinling should
be the *Very Special Guests*.

NOTICE BOARD

THE LIGHTHOUSE BIRTHDAY CELEBRATION 200 YEARS OLD

- VERY SPECIAL GUESTS: MR + MRS GRINLING
- ALL NIGHT SEA PARTY FOLLOWED BY A BIRTHDAY BREAKFAST
- PLEASE WEAR FANCY DRESS

RSVP: SALLY DE LA CROISSANT

It was so difficult to choose the best fancy dress.
"Shall I wear the shark suit?" asked Mr Grinling.
"Could I be a mermaid?" wondered Mrs Grinling.
But when they discovered the pirate costumes
their minds were quite made up.

"All my life I've yearned to be a pirate,"
sighed Mrs Grinling. "To spit and swear
and roam the seven seas."
"And search for treasure on a treasure
island," added Mr Grinling.
"We'll be splendid pirates," cried
Mrs Grinling as she swashed and
buckled around the room.
"Hattie and Herbert, the scourge
of the seven seas."

"Oo-aargh!" said Mr Grinling and he
swashed and buckled too.
"Perhaps Hamish could be our pirate cat,"
suggested Mrs Grinling.
But Hamish had very different ideas.

Whenever Mrs Grinling wanted
him to try his pirate costume,
Hamish disappeared.
"Drat that cat," she
exclaimed. "Where does
he go these days?"

The Grinlings practised being pirates at every opportunity.

Here's yer toast, me olde one-eyed beauty.

Ooh-arrgh!

SWASH!

Avast, me hearties – let's stir the crow's nest soup . . .

But Mr Grinling's cutlass caused all sorts of difficulties.

Shiver me timbers!! Careful, Captain!

R-R-I-P!!

Yoggle the yardarm . . .

CLUNK!!

"I do want to be a pirate," he said sadly. "I'm just not very good at it. Perhaps I should have gone as a shark after all."

Mrs Grinling quite frightened Sam and the seagulls with her cursing and swearing.

On the night of the party the Grinlings rowed out towards the party ship. At first its lights shone clearly across the water but gradually they dimmed and soon they vanished altogether.

"What can have happened, Mrs G?" said Mr Grinling. "We can't be lost."
The waves slapped against the little boat. It was darker than Mr Grinling
had ever seen it. And then as the lighthouse flashed across the bay . . .

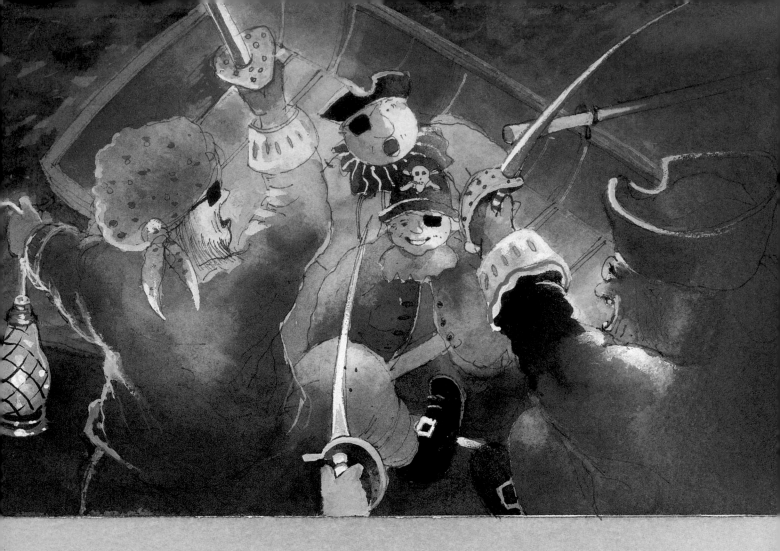

"Look, Mr G!" exclaimed Mrs Grinling. "Someone to rescue us."
A speed boat swished in beside them nearly swamping the little dinghy.
Three pirates leapt across the bow and thrust their shining cutlasses
in the air.
"Oo-aargh!" they roared and they rampaged round the dinghy.
Mrs Grinling was delighted.
"Real pirates," she whispered to Mr Grinling and she forgot all about
the Sea Party.

"Oo-aargh," growled the fiercest pirate. "We be pirates and this be our
pirate patch. We're on the look-out for likely new recruits."

"Oh, yes!" exclaimed Mrs Grinling. "We'd love to be pirates.
Yo-ho-ho and a bottle of rum."
Mr Grinling waved his cutlass rather feebly.
The pirates appeared rather surprised.
"'Course, you have to show us that you can be pirates,"
snarled the smallest and smelliest pirate.
"You have to pass the Incredibly Difficult Pirate Tests."
Mr Grinling wasn't sure about pirate tests.
"OK lads," shouted the fiercest pirate. "We'll blindfold 'em and gag 'em
and take 'em back to the Captain. She'll soon find out if they're made of
proper pirate material, you all know what she's like."

The pirate captain was a particularly nasty-looking piece of work. She had black teeth and smelt of rotten fish and seaweed. A grubby white parrot clung to her shoulder.

"Right, me hearties, what have we 'ere?" She peg-legged around the Grinlings. "So you want to join our pirate crew?"

"Oh yes, please," said Mrs Grinling.
"Definitely," agreed Mr Grinling.
"Well, you look like pirates and you smell like pirates but you have to pass the six pirate tests before you can be pirates. Are you ready?" asked the Captain. "So what comes first, me hearties?"

"The Swearing Test!" shouted the pirates.
Mrs Grinling swore loud and long.
The parrot covered his ears.
Mr Grinling thought for a while.
"Blithering bumbollards," he muttered at last.
The pirates shook their heads.

"Now the Sleeping in a Hammock in a Force Nine Gale Test.
Rock that ship, me bully boys and girls."
Mrs Grinling held tightly to the hammock sides and smiled happily.
Mr Grinling bounced right out of his hammock and was seasick
several times.
The pirates groaned.

"The Jolly Roger Flag Test," shouted Captain Bosibelle.
"Just a quick climb to the crow's-nest."
Mrs Grinling scampered up the rope ladder. At the top she not only
hoisted the flag but waved her cutlass.
"Shiver me timbers!" shouted the pirates.

Mr Grinling closed his eyes as he started to climb.
"Don't look down," he muttered to himself. "Think of Hamish and Sam.
Think of nice things to eat, Peach Surprise and iced sea biscuits, think
of-ah-ah-ah . . ."

He fell into a barrel of foul-smelling water.
"I'm so sorry," said the Captain.
"They're very polite for pirates," spluttered Mr Grinling to Mrs Grinling.

TREASURE MAP

CODE: dvbw szlgd wbbu
bu dvz1 hck k dvb azb
iku cikh1lz yintez pgi
ihpcv oitu dp vfdlz dzzit

"Pirate Test number four," announced Captain Bosibelle.

"Finding the Treasure," roared all the pirates.

"Here's the map," said Captain Bosibelle.

"There's lovely treasure hidden on our ship, you've got ten minutes to find it."

"Oo-aargh," shouted the Grinlings and off they raced.

OUTSIDE LOO

Off we go, Hattie – not much time!

Up we go . . .

Quickly, Hattie . .

Nothing here.

Oh dear!

This is empty.

CODE:
When all seems
All can be won.
A surprise awai
Under somebod

Herbert – I've cracked the code!!

When all seems lost,
All can be won.
A surprise awaits,
Under somebody's . . .

They found the treasure chest under the bottom of a very small pirate. "Open sesame!" shouted the pirates. The chest was big enough for only one jewel and two pieces of eight. "We're a little short of treasure at the moment," explained the Captain. "No decent raids lately."

"And now the most dangerous, the most terrifying, the most dastardly test of them all."

"Eating Pirate Food!" shouted the pirates.

"Eating," said Mr Grinling happily. "Now eating is something I can do."

Some of the smaller pirates sniggered.

Captain Bosibelle laid out the food. Two maggots and a weevil wriggled across the biscuit. Mrs Grinling turned quite green but Mr Grinling ate it, weevils, maggots and all.

"Hurrah," cheered the pirates.

"And now number six, the final test. If you pass this you can join our
pirate gang. Tell 'em, me bouncing buccaneers."
"Walking the Plank," cried the pirates.
"Oh," said Mrs Grinling.
"Dearie me," said Mr Grinling.
The water below looked smoothly dark and menacing. Mr Grinling
wished he was wearing the shark costume.
"Do you think I could ask for arm bands?" he whispered.
Mrs Grinling looked at the pirates' faces and shook her head.

"We've always wanted to be pirates, Mr G," she said. "We aren't afraid of a little bit of water, are we?"

"Goodness, no," said Mr Grinling.

But his knees knocked and his tummy felt all wobbly like a jelly.

"Ready," he said and he held his nose.

"Steady," said Mrs Grinling and she closed her eyes.

"Just a minute," said Mr Grinling, letting go of his nose.

"Something's amiss here. Whoever heard of new pirates walking the plank? We could drown before we've done any pirating."

Suddenly the pirates pulled off their disguises.
"Surprise, surprise," they shouted.
The Grinlings were so astounded
they nearly fell into the water.
"Jason the postman!" exclaimed Mr Grinling.

"Admiral Fleetabix!" cried
Mrs Grinling.
"And Sally de la Croissant!"
they said both together.

"We heard how you longed to be pirates,"
she explained. "So we planned a
Pirate Experience. We had to be nasty
so you'd think we were real."
"We certainly did," said Mr Grinling
as he mopped his brow.

The lighthouse beamed its last light across the bay.
"It's party time," called Jason the postman.
He picked up his fiddle and started to play.
"May I have the pleasure, Pirate Herbert?" asked Mrs Grinling.
"Oo-aargh! Pirate Hattie," smiled Mr Grinling.
And they all danced until they could dance no more.

"Sun's up!" called Sally de la Croissant.
"Time for the birthday breakfast."
Mrs Grinling looked worried.
"We can't have the party without Hamish."
"Or Sam," said Mr Grinling.

Q: Why is
Mr Grinling
like a fish?

A: Because
he's a dear
old sole!

"They're coming, they're coming!" shouted the children. "Just in time for the food," said Sam as he climbed on to the deck. He placed a large, wicker basket at the Grinlings' feet and carefully opened the lid.
Out jumped . . .

Hamish and Mrs Hamish and four little Hamishes.

"Now that's what I call real treasure," smiled Mr Grinling.